CW00866114

A pony's tale

Written by Jennifer Story
Illustrated by Ben Nathan Story

For Arthur

Other books by Jennifer Story & Ben Nathan Story:
Chiltern Valley Sundays, 16 routes for cyclists (1996)
ISBN 1-898073-08-2

Other books from Leveret Press:
The Trouble with Harry by Jack Trevor Story (1985)
ISBN 0 947856 00 5
Dwarf Goes to Oxford by Jack Trevor Story (1987)
ISBN 0 947856 021

© Jennifer Story 2016

All rights reserved
No part of this publication may be produced, stored in a retrieval system,
or transmitted in any form or by any means (electronic, mechanical,
photocopying, recording or otherwise) without prior permission of the
copyright holder.

Publisher's note
While this book aims at a true representation of life in the New Forest
and refers to traditional forest names and actual place names for its
settings, any characterisation of persons or animals is purely imaginary
and any similarities to such are unintentional.

Published by:
Leveret Press
www.leveretpress.com

Contents

The New Forest has a language of its own.
See how many words you can count in the story
that you haven't heard before.

Natives of the Forest

Thousands of ponies live in the wild in the *New Forest*. They have been here since the time when medieval kings and their noblemen used the forest as a hunting ground.

Riding on the backs of strong, fast horses they chased deer and *wild boar* for miles across the heathland and through the woods, leaping over streams and fallen trees, and sometimes galloping into a *peat bog,* where the horses' legs would get covered in dark mud.

The commotion scattered the other wild animals who fled in fear for their lives.

Nowadays, the ponies and the deer have a quieter life. They graze on the *lawns* amongst the bracken and heather, and drink from natural streams and ponds.

Sometimes cows and pigs join them and roam the *open forest* searching for food, but the *cattle grids*

stop them straying away from their forest home.

In the Winter when the grass stops growing, the ponies snack on prickly holly leaves and even spiky *gorse bushes*! When it snows, some *commoners* will take a bale of hay out onto the forest and leave it for their ponies.

The ponies soon learn where their owner lives and will gather by the gate, hoping for an extra helping of hay on cold mornings.

Some mares will spend many years of their lives in the wild. Each spring there will be new foals who will learn the ways of the forest from their mothers and grand-mothers.

The *agisters* who work here look after all the animals to make sure there will be ponies in the New Forest for hundreds of years to come.

Apart from ponies, what other animals might
you see living in the New Forest?

1

Whispering Trees

From her rug next to the Aga, in a farmhouse deep in the Forest, Flo the sheepdog can hear something stirring.

She pricks up one of her ears and lifts her head. Flo looks at the world through one pale blue eye and one dark brown one, but she can see and hear and smell as well as any dog. Something isn't quite right and a grumbling growl starts in her throat.

'What's up with you?' Tanya sits at her farmhouse table, weaving a basket from bulrushes and dogwood stems.

'It'll be those witches out on the Down' says her husband Tom in a teasing voice, 'dancing around one of their witchy circles and casting their wizardy spells'.

'Rubbish!' Tanya snorts. 'Just because its a Full Moon doesn't mean the Forest is full of witches! Anyway, if there ARE any they'll be white witches and friendly, won't they Flo?'

Flo stops growling, lowers her head back onto her paws and wags her tail once or twice in agreement before closing her one brown eye again. It isn't witches or warlocks or Full Moons on her mind - it's something else.

The Forest has been whispering to her that changes are afoot, and she'll know soon enough what's up.

But humans don't understand these things.

They can't see or smell or hear as well as an old sheepdog with one *wall eye* can.

Out on the forest the ponies and deer and foxes and rabbits and cows and badgers have heard the whisper. They linger in the shadows of the tall pine trees that stand in rows like soldiers.

The Moon's silvery reflection wobbles in the ponds and streams with an eerie light. The air is so still you could hear a pine needle drop, but it carries a sweet scent that makes the ponies' nostrils twitch.

Nights are getting shorter and the bright green bracken is beginning to uncurl itself, and this can only mean it's Spring. All the wild animals know that magic is about to happen.

*   *   *   *

Merrill is a pretty *bay* pony with eyes so dark and shiny they look like pebbles from the sea bed. She belongs to a small herd of mares that live in a big hollow below Acres Down. Here they find many things to eat - holly, gorse, broom, bracken and coarse marsh grass.

On the top of the gravelly hill above the hollow, the heather grows in clumps. Away across the tree tops on a clear day, you can see the Isle of Wight.

The day after the night of the full Moon, shafts of May sunshine dance amongst the branches. The ponies are resting beside a circle of holly bushes, swishing their tails at a few annoying gnats and nodding their heads in the gentle breeze.

Merrill is about to give birth. She has carried her unborn foal in her tummy for nearly a year, and senses that her little one will soon arrive in the world. Her sister, Faye, is also ready to give birth.

Faye is a light chestnut pony with a shaggy mane and tail the colour of butter. Her last foal was taken away to become a riding pony and she misses the little dappled grey colt. Faye won't be lonely any more when her new foal arrives.

The warm weather brings lots of visitors to the New Forest and at noon, several people ramble past the little group at Acres Down. They pause to admire the pretty mares and notice the two with fat tummies.

'Those two will be dropping their foals any day now', says a large man with binoculars. He's hoping to spot the *Goshawk* that's known to have a nest nearby.

Next, a chattering family comes along, looking for the perfect place to have their picnic. 'Over here!' points the boy, and he flaps a big tartan rug over the short grass and lays it flat.

Several creamy-coloured cows lazing in the sun watch the unpacking of the picnic basket with faraway eyes and mouths that never stop chewing.

In the afternoon, Merrill becomes restless. She seeks a quiet place away from the rest of the herd and lays down under an oak tree.

Her body feels heavy and she gazes around at her friends with a look that says: 'The time is near, keep your distance.'

But Faye's looking out for Merrill. She stands on a little mound, scanning the horizon for any sign of danger.

All the people have long since gone on their way. For the time being, the forest is calm and safe.

By evening, poor Merrill is feeling quite uncomfortable. She gets up and paces around, making little *whinnying* sounds.

From her position by the holly bushes, Faye keeps watch. As the sun sinks low over the pine trees, Acres Down is cloaked in gentle twilight. The air turns cool and silky again.

And then suddenly a shrill whinny rips the silence apart and echoes around the hollow. Lots of animal ears prick up. Lots of eyes turn towards the *copse*. Here it comes! The thing we've been waiting for!

Merrill cries out in a moment of pain and then, a few moments later, at her feet is a new foal. It's a little *filly*.

The wild animals frisk and play. The first foal of Spring! New life has come to the Forest! Flo barks joyously from her rug by the Aga.

As her own mother did at Merrill's birth, and her grandmother before her, the weary mare licks the foal clean and feels a need to protect her.

The little filly is a light bay with a white *flash* the length of her face. Her deep blue eyes are shielded by long black eyelashes as she watches her mother leaning over her.

The others in the herd shuffle closer to have a look. In the dark, the flash on the foal's face is as bright as the moon.

It's only an hour before she tries to stand on her thin shaky legs. She nudges her mother's belly to find the sweet milk there to feed her.

The little foal's legs are so long she won't be able to reach the ground with her head to eat grass for several weeks!

But a bond quickly forms with her mother so she can drink the mare's milk as often as she needs.

They have a long night to get to know each other well.

By dawn, the herd has wandered down the hill towards the car park, to warm up after a night under the trees.

Already, a Land Rover's bumping along the track, its fat tyres making clouds of dust.

As soon as it has squealed to a stop, a young girl with long brown pigtails opens the door, ready to jump out.
'I see her, Dad! She's got her foal!'

In her excitement, Ruby forgets to let Flo out of the back of the Land Rover. The collie whines and scratches to get free, her wet nose pressed to the window and her oddly coloured eyes staring out.

Knowing how protective Merrill will be of her new foal, Ruby approaches slowly, treading as softly on the ground as she can and hardly daring to breathe.

'Hey Merrill, good girl', she whispers, and her mare recognises the kind commoner girl and looks at her with calm eyes. 'What a clever pony you are!' whispers Ruby, seeing how perfect the little foal looks. 'Can we meet your new baby?'

Ruby and her Dad move as close to the foal as Merrill will allow so they can see that she's OK and that the birth was normal. 'It's a filly! She's a pretty one that's for sure', says Tom.

At the sound of his gruff voice, the foal skips round to the other side of her mother to hide. Tom and his daughter laugh as she peeps out at them from the shelter of her mother's flank.

Meanwhile, clever Flo has leapt over into the front seat of the Land Rover and escaped through the open window. She sniffs the air which is ruffled with the scent of mare's milk and May blossom, but then she stops in her tracks with one paw raised.

The whisper has started again in the high branches. Flo hears Ruby take a deep breath as she comes to a decision.

'You will be called Blaze', she tells the foal, 'because of your bright white flash!'

Merrill swishes her tail to keep her little one close and nods her head, as if to say, 'that's a good name for my foal.'

If you stand with your feet wide apart, can you reach the ground with your head?

Rabbits and Rainbows

In her new surroundings, there's so much for Blaze to take in.

At just a few days old, she hears her first cuckoo singing near Crown Wood. Her head goes up, her eyes pop wide, and with ears pricked she listens in wonder to the clear call, sounding over and over like a bell in the still air.

But try as she might, she can't make the same sound. She hasn't found her proper voice yet and can only make a sort of snorting noise through her wide nostrils.

When Tom sets out in his hiking boots at the weekend, Blaze spies him heading along the track towards the hollow where the ponies are gathered.

There's something small scurrying at his feet, sometimes black and sometimes white. Curious, Blaze trots a short way up the hill on her dainty hooves to have a closer look. She comes to a sudden halt and jumps out of her skin as the small thing lets out a loud WOOF!

Spinning round, she canters back to her mother's side, puffing and panting in fright. Merrill hardly looks up. She has seen Flo many times and knows that's just the way she says Hello.

In the second week, the ponies wander through the heather to a favourite spot called the Witches Pool, where five black cows are wading.

The water is bright blue under the cloudless sky. The ponies put their faces down to the surface of the pond to drink, and Blaze shyly mimics them.

But the sight of a bright white streak, shimmering in the water just beneath her *muzzle*, startles her. She leaps from the pond's edge splashing water all over herself and the other ponies and the five black cows.

Her friends continue to drink calmly, and the cattle take no notice. After a little while, Blaze is brave enough to come back and look again. The strange white streak is still dancing there and now it has big nostrils and gleaming eyes!

Gingerly, she puts her face closer, so her nose is nearly touching the nose in the pool, and tries a sip, drawing the cool fresh water up into her mouth and down her throat. She dribbles droplets happily from her long pink tongue. It tastes and feels so good!

And the face in the pond has disappeared amongst the ripples.

Towards the end of the third week, bubbly grey clouds bring her first sudden rain shower and a whistling gust of wind shakes cold splodges from the leaves straight down onto Blaze's head. She shudders off the water from her tufty mane. Why is she always getting wet?

Next, Blaze is bewildered by a badger shuffling slowly through old rotting leaves and surprised at a squirrel suddenly shooting up a tree beside her.

But the thing that puzzles her most is the rabbit that pops its head out of a hole at her feet. And then just as quickly disappears.

Blaze spins round to try and see where it has vanished to and when she turns back - there it is again! But only for a split second and then - pfff! gone without a trace.

It's a game of hide and seek that amuses and perplexes Blaze at the same time. For she's afraid to peer down the rabbit hole in case she falls in and is never seen again.

Now the foal is a month old. She's getting to know the world around her as Merrill watches with pride. Nature is full of surprises and the magical forest casts new spells every day. These are exciting times for both Blaze and her mother.

In the meantime, Faye has also given birth. The dark bay foal is born a few days after Blaze. His coat is soft and fuzzy and his short mane stands up like a brush.

He is shy and gentle and stays close to his mother's side, peeping out at Blaze, and watching with eyes like saucers as she investigates fox holes, dips her nose and hooves into ponds and streams, and has fun stretching her legs with a swift gallop across the grass.

Too timid to venture any distance from Faye, the new foal learns quickly how to eat like she does, nibbling grass, bracken and leaves. Although his legs are still too long to allow his head to reach the ground, he finds that if he stands in a ditch, the lush grass at the top of the bank is easy to get to.

In the shifting shadows of a bright Spring day, the little *colt* suddenly finds himself left behind the others. They've quietly headed away from the car park to the shelter of the copse. He's all alone!
Quivering with fear he shies and slips on the

gravel track and nearly does the splits! But then he sees a face watching him from the woodland clearing.

The *fallow deer* is just as surprised to see the fuzzy little foal as he is to see a creature with such big ears and eyes standing like a statue in front of him. But they like the look of each other and are rather pleased to meet.

The deer holds the foal's gaze and then calmly turns and heads slowly up the path, bruising the blue dog violets at her feet so that they give off their pretty scent. She turns now and then to see if her new friend is following.

The foal is right behind, fascinated by the deer's fluffy black and white tail which bobs ahead of him in and out of the bracken.

At the top of the path, the deer gives him one last look and then gracefully bounds away. As the foal watches her go, he spots his mother in the distant hollow and lets out a cry. Faye calls back with her familiar *nickering* neigh. Without hesitation, her little one scurries back to the warmth and safety of her side.

But despite the odd scary accident, occasional drenchings, and creatures that keep disappearing, both Blaze and her fuzzy friend are beginning to feel at home in the forest. Day by day they're learning that most animals are harmless and most adventures are fun.

It's the ponies' commoner owners who have a problem. What are they going to call Faye's little foal?

'Bear', says Tanya 'because he's fuzzy like Ruby's old teddy!'
'I like Rocco', muses Tom as he whittles a piece of spiny oak branch into a candle holder. 'Or Louie. I used to have a donkey called Louie'.
'Its still not quite right Dad', Ruby chips in. 'Maybe a really good name will pop into our heads that'll suit him perfectly.'

Flo already knows what the foal will be called as she can see into the future with her one pale blue eye. She barks to tell everyone, but to them it's just a bark.

'Can we go up and see them later, Dad?' Ruby begs. Tom looks out of the window towards the Down. 'We'll go after lunch. Looks like a heavy shower's coming', he says and sits down at the table, just as the rain starts plopping onto the path outside.

And that's how it happens that the foal gets his name. For after their lunch Tom and Ruby put on their rain jackets and boots and climb the track towards the top of the Down, where the last drops of the rain shower spatter through the branches of the trees.

The ponies are on the top of the hill looking out across the heath towards the Isle of Wight, to where the dark clouds are retreating.

In the boughs above their heads, sparkling raindrops hang like diamonds from the leaves. It's a glittering wonderland to the little foals.

'The sun's coming out!' smiles Ruby and skips along at her Dad's side happily in the warm brightness, being careful not to approach the ponies too fast or it will scare the foals.

'Hey look Ruby!' declares Tom. 'A rainbow!' And sure enough, they watch as a vivid band of colours paints a giant arch across the sky.

'That's it Dad!' Ruby claps her hands and then has to apologise to the little fuzzy brown foal for frightening him. 'We'll call him Rainbow - or Bo for short!'.

'Bo - I like that', agrees Tom.
'Yep Yep Yep!' barks Flo. At last they've got it!

Can you make the sound of a cuckoo?

Try drinking through a straw. This is the same way that a pony sucks up water from a pond or stream!

3

Bitten!

There are trickling springs, babbling brooks and rushing streams criss-crossing the New Forest everywhere. Sometimes the rivulets run right over the road and you have to drive through a *ford;* sometimes there'll be a wooden bridge where you can get across.

A few of the bridges are wide and strong enough to bear the weight of a carriage pulled by two big horses and with four passengers on board.

On a hot afternoon in July, Millyford bridge is crowded with a group of children from the Activity Centre.

They're learning about the plants, the insects and the reptiles that live in the *Inclosure.*

Leading the group is Mr Findlow who knows lots of interesting facts about the Forest. He's also full of good ideas. As the children look down into the clear stream below, he suddenly claps his hands together and suggests: 'How about a game? Let's race some twigs in the stream!'

Everyone gets busy looking for suitably small sticks and snapping them into floatable sizes. Bits of broken twig spin down into the stream from the wooden railings. Then the children rush to the other side to see whose is first under the bridge.

There hasn't been any rain lately and the stream's running quite slowly, but the children soon discover that the twigs that float in the middle of the stream are the quickest to appear on the other side.

'I've won!' 'I'VE won!' 'No that's MY stick', call out several children all at once.

'I judge Sam Penny to be the winner!' declares Mr Findlow. 'Now I'm going to get the next task ready. You'll each need a jam jar to take some water samples.'

Merrill and Faye's herd are watching and listening from the other side of the stream. While they linger in the cool glade, their tails are swishing constantly. Clouds of midges revolve dizzily amongst them, mzz-ing in their ears.

There's another rare and strange type of fly that lives in the forest and loves annoying ponies! They land on the backs of the surprised animals and then scuttle sideways to burrow under their hair. They're looking for a nice patch of warm skin to bite.

The ponies can't catch these flies with their teeth because they're too quick, and they can't squash them by rubbing against a tree or rolling on the ground because they have very hard shells. That's why they're known as *Crab flies*.

This afternoon, it's bad luck for the ponies that there's a crab fly nest nearby. A swirling swarm lands on the warm coats of Blaze and Bo like a rash of black spots. Then the creepy creatures start scuttling round to their underbellies. The foals feel them tickling and pricking them, but without arms and hands they can't even scratch. It's unbearable!

Meanwhile, the midges have moved to the other bank of the stream and are slyly biting at the bare arms of the boys and girls as they dip their jam jars into the water.

At the 'Ow-owws!' of the children and the 'Yeee-hees!' of the foals - who have certainly found their voices now - Mr Findlow drops his folder and looks up through misty glasses. 'Whaaaat?' he murmurs in disbelief. There are red-faced children twisting and squirming and scratching, and ponies bucking and leaping - it looks like a crazy dance routine!

'Oh dear, I'd better get out some spray', he mutters, rummaging deep in his rucksack.

With wild eyes, sweaty manes and flying tails, Bo and Blaze are still prancing on the spot long after the children have moved on through the trees, with their jars slopping murky liquid and arms covered in pink spots.

It will be several hours before the crab flies will

fly off again. Until then it will be a very tickly time for the two foals!

They're not the only ones to be uncomfortable out on the Forest today. About a mile away, on the lane to Bolderwood, another small herd of ponies has gathered near the roadside where there's a shallow pool of water. They've stopped to enjoy a refreshing drink.

Just then a bright orange camper van pulls up at the side of the lane and a Mum, Dad, Grandpa and two children tumble out to take selfies with the ponies.

The girl clutches a foil packet and pulls out a big yellow crisp to pop into her mouth. She decides the pretty *roan* pony watching her from the edge of the pool must be hungry too. It's only got short grass to eat.

She sidles up to the pony, unnoticed by her Mum and Dad, and offers the cheesy disc to the pony, waving it close to her face.

"Owwwww!' Her parents look round from their camera phones to see what's happened. 'It bit my finger!' wails the little girl, her face red and tears bouncing down her cheeks.

'You should be more careful with wild animals,' her Grandpa tells her gently. 'They're not the same as riding school ponies you know.'
'I don't like ponies anymore,' she snuffles, rubbing her hand.

Heading off again in their shiny van, her brother's already on Facebook uploading a great photo of his sister being bitten by a pony. 'Maybe it prefers salt and vinegar flavour!' he sniggers. The girl gives him a shove and he shoves her back.

'Stop it you two', shouts their Dad for the umpteenth time today, and in the hullabaloo nobody notices as they pass a large sign at the edge of the road that says: 'Please do not feed the ponies. They can bite!'

Nor do the people queueing for ice creams at Bolderwood notice the sun-baked snake that uncoils itself slowly and slithers silently away under the heather. He simply can't be bothered to bite anybody today.

Have you ever played the twig race game? Next time you're on a bridge over a stream have a go.

And remember not to feed the New Forest ponies!

4

A Summer Trail

After their fun with the flies, Blaze and Bo are special friends. They still keep close to their mothers when they want to feed, but when they feel brave enough, they explore a little further away from the herd, calling out if they lose sight of the older ponies.

This quickly brings up the mares' heads and they whinny back so Bo and Blaze can follow the sound and return to safety.

But in the dark velvety night of the New Moon, it's easier for the foals to lose their way.

Especially out on White Moor. This is a bleak and lonely place in the dark, with just a thin watery ditch running through the middle and thick black woods all round the edges.

While the foals are investigating the banks of the ditch, the others have drifted off to the cover of the trees. No one replies to the foals' calls. Their ears prick and their nerves twitch as they realise they could be in danger.

Trotting towards the edge of the moor on hooves so light they hardly make a sound, Bo hops over some pieces of broken wood on the ground and finds himself standing in the middle of a circle. It's made of old gnarled branches from the dead oak tree, which seem to have been laid carefully end-to-end to form a perfect ring.

He's wandered into a *witches' circle!* In his panic to get out Bo scatters some of the branches and breaks the ring. Oops! It's supposed to be unlucky to spoil a witches' circle!

And then - WHOOSH! With a sudden rush of air and a ghostly woo-ing noise, something swoops above Bo's head and settles in the branch of a tall beech tree. The little foal can just make out a white shape perched high above his path and it seems to be watching and waiting for him.

Bo stands rooted to the spot, not daring to breathe. For the creature has a luminous face as blank as a sheet but for two black seeds for eyes and a sharp curved thorn for a nose. Then the weirdest thing happens.

Bo watches in horror as the Thing's head swivels right round on its neck in one smooth turn - and that's enough to get the foal galloping again, off into the black woods. He tears along Blaze's newly-trodden track through the brambles and bracken. He should never have stepped on the witches' circle!

Back with the herd, the foals huddle together. The night wraps its cool cloak silently around them and they doze beneath the stars.

The spooks have disappeared back into the dark shadows and they feel safe again.

Quietly the older ponies take turns to watch and listen, some asleep on their feet, others laying down on a soft bed of bracken and leaf mould. Then, after a few hours, the sky over the far side of the moor turns light blue, then yellow with golden streaks of pink, just ahead of the rising sun.

Birds start singing from the high branches and after an hour or so, the first shafts of sunlight prick through the canopy of leaves above the ponies' heads.

Blaze twitches her nose and Bo flicks an ear. The mares snort and smack their lips and several show off their long yellow teeth and pink gums as a big yawn spreads through the herd. It's a new morning on the moor and the forest slowly wakens.

* * * *

By high summer, the young foals are growing fast and getting more hungry and thirsty. They follow the herd further afield up onto Stoney Cross and down to Withybed Bottom where they're disappointed to find only a trickle of water in the streams and ditches.

Many of their familiar ponds have shrunk to shallow puddles. Some have dried up completely and turned to dust under the hot sun.

They search everywhere for fresh grass and something to drink.

Blaze is so thirsty! Standing in a dry river bed she sees a tiny creature crawling through the cracks in the earth to where some coarse grass grows in tufts. The tufts are dotted all over the ground like cushions, hiding a much darker, softer mud.

Blaze follows the wriggling reptile with her nose until it plops under the sloppy wet mud and all that's left is a few bubbles on the surface. Blaze gives them a sniff and they burst in her face.

As she jumps away the ground seems to move beneath her and she hops onto the green cushions to try and get her balance. But even they seem to be floating on a very wobbly jelly. Blaze's legs slip and slide beneath her. She's adrift over a deep bog!

Her cries bring Merrill, Faye and Bo to have a look. Bo bounces up and down on a clump of *Bog*

Myrtle in his excitement and in her panic Blaze starts bouncing too - right off her tufts into the thick mud.

Using all her strength, she pounds at the mire with her front hooves and manages to pull her hind legs free. Bo gallops round in fright as his friend makes a giant leap for solid ground.

Exhausted, frightened and covered in mud she stands shakily at the edge of the bog with Bo. Her coat is now the same colour as his and even her white blaze has disappeared under the *peat* splatters.

Bo breathes in the earthy smell of the black mud on Blaze's face and she blows back into his nostrils so he'll know for sure it's really her.

The older ponies turn away now the danger has passed. They can sniff out a bog by the smell of peat under the water. They put their heads down to the surface so they can sense how deep and dangerous it might be, before daring to tread on it.

Oh well, Blaze will learn eventually!

The heatwave lasts for two weeks. The days seem endless and the ponies look forward to sunset when the shadows lengthen and the bees and wasps leave the scented air to bumble off to their secret nests. This is a favourite time for Blaze and Bo.

Sometimes on these evenings they see their commoner friends, Tanya and Ruby riding their tame ponies across the Down. Flo runs ahead, disappearing under the bracken now and then to investigate an interesting smell. The herd watch with sleepy eyes, listening to the humans chatter as they disappear into the distance and the softening light.

*   *   *   *

August turns the forest into a landscape of pink and purple. The heather has flowered all over the heathlands. There are nuts and berries in the hedgerows and young green acorns on the oak trees. Brambles tumble over *briars*, covered in shining blackberries, and trees hang heavy, laden with yellow crab apples.

Merrill and Faye look at the acorns dangling from the oak tree with wary eyes, and Blaze and Bo wonder what could be wrong with this harmless looking fruit. Don't they taste as good as the beechnuts that they find inside their spiky shells? They stretch their necks to investigate the glossy orange berries of a Rowan and the reddening clusters on the Holly bush.

The turning of the season is kind to the ponies. The flies are less bothersome and the traffic slows. With the end of the holidays, the crowds have melted away and the ponies and other wildlife have the quiet forest all to themselves again. Well, nearly.

The forest rangers come by from time to time, tidying the verges and setting small fires to burn old roots and dead branches. The smoke from their fires drifts upwards here and there, leaving grey wisps on the horizon.

And Tom comes along the track in his hiking boots, often with friends by his side and always with Flo at his heels.

Can you guess which creature it was that Bo saw in the branches?

How many different colours might you see on the forest in August?

5

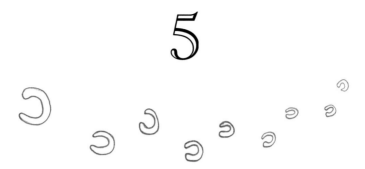

The Day of the Drift

'You two'll need a good breakfast today!' declares Tanya as she prods and turns the bacon rashers and fat sausages sizzling under the grill.

Make that three! thinks Flo as she sniffs the air with her shiny black nose.

They're all going to need a good meal inside them for this is the day when they're off to round up the ponies of the forest, so they can be checked over and counted.

Tom and Ruby are hungry and Flo only gets thrown a scrap of bacon rind when they're finished, which isn't enough for an old sheepdog with a big appetite. When Tom scrapes his chair back and goes off to the yard, two front paws appear on the table and a long tongue licks greedily at the smear of egg yolk and brown sauce left on his plate.

Tom chooses a saddle and two bridles from the tack room and helps Ruby get her pony Muffin ready. Tom only needs a bridle for his mare Connie. He's going to ride bare back for the *Drift*.

Flo comes out of the back door still licking at her greasy nose and jogs across the yard to catch up with Ruby and Muffin. They set off together for Withybed Bottom. There's a *pound* there where all the rounded-up ponies will be held, and Ruby always helps with the gates.

From Acres Down to Stoney Cross and from Bolderwood to Emery Down, the round-up riders are getting ready for a busy day. They're out and about on their ponies everywhere, trotting down the tracks and lanes to their gathering place on Pilmore Heath.

'Right' cries Rob Sweet who's ridden many drifts before. 'Let's get going everyone. Now don't let any of 'em get away. We want to see the whole lot up in the pound at Withybed by lunch time!'

Down in the hollow, Blaze and Bo are getting fidgety. There's a tingle in the air that tells them something's not right and the message seems to pass from pony to pony, herd to herd, region to region across the forest.

Some animals snort and whinny, others shy at the faintest crackle of a broken twig. Even the rustle of a leaf falling through the branches of the big beech tree makes them jumpy.

When one or two ponies come cantering by, all of Merrill's herd follow and its the same all over the Down and heath, until there are lots of little stampedes gathering pace through the woods and across the plain.

Commoners on horseback are coming from all directions and soon every wild pony in this part of the forest is on the run.

Most of the riders taking part in the round-up are young men from local farms, mounted on their own *New Foresters* and many are riding bareback like Tom.

They are fast and fit and they've been taking part in the drifts since they were boys. As they gallop along, the men sit tight on the ponies' backs shouting to each other and urging one another to go faster, laughing as they pick up speed.

Manes flying and sweat foaming on their necks, their keen mounts are excited and going at full gallop. They know what job they have to do.

Two riders close in on the herd as they canter up the side of the hill, trying to escape. Blaze and Bo are in the middle of them, running for their lives. Are they being chased from their haunt, never to return? All they know is - they just have to get away!

But the riders are quick and skilful and drive their *quarry* along the ridge towards the pound where they can pen them in. They position themselves either side of the fleeing ponies and squeeze them into line.

Suddenly the wild herds see fencing and gates ahead of them and they start to panic. They're going to be trapped! As they race towards the wooden rails of the corral they swerve dangerously away. It's their last chance to avoid capture.

But a pair of bullying collies yelp and snarl at their heels, determined to keep the stampede in line. They drive the ponies back into the rails, straight through the opening and into the pens.

Ruby hangs over one of the wooden gates, ready to snap it shut once all the animals are in the pound. 'Ok Ruby, close them in!' shouts Rob Sweet from the side of the corral and Ruby jumps from the gate and slams it into the latch with a clunk.

She's tied Muffin's reins around a post a little way off, so her gentle mare won't get caught up in the hustle and bustle of the pens, and where the scuffling dogs and shouting commoners can't worry her.

Max, from Ruby's village school, is there too, in the middle of the crowd. He's got some shiny conkers tied on strings. 'Want a game?' he asks

Ruby, handing her his biggest and shiniest conker.

She tries to swing it at his which is spinning on the end of its string, but misses. She hears her conker crack against Max's knuckles. 'Ow!' he says. 'You're meant to hit the conker not me!' 'Sorry Max!'

Flo stalks around in the middle of the crowd, with her head down and tail quivering. She doesn't like those sharp eyed dogs. She'd jump on them and roll them over if she could!

Blaze and Bo stand panting in the pound. They're worn out and sweaty and their ribs rise and fall quickly with each breath.

One by one all the ponies are approached by the men and women of the drift. 'Come here young fella' wheezes an older man, out of breath. He has a rope in his bony hands. He slips it swiftly round the neck of a startled Bo.

The commoners handle their captives gently and easily, having been used to the wild ponies all their lives. They have to check the health of each one, worm them, brand the new ones to show who they belong to, and clip the tails of others in a particular way, to show which part of the forest they belong to.

'This one's got a tail like spun gold!' says a young woman to her friend. 'Such a shame to cut it!' 'Can I take the hair home Mum?' asks Max's sister Poppy. She holds the clippings from Faye's tail carefully in her hand as if they're strands from a moonbeam.

The young ponies squeal as the branding iron scorches their backs but it's over quickly and they're soon released from the crowded pen. They buck and whinny with joy as they're returned to the open plain.

Merrill and Faye have old scars that spell 'TT' on their backs as they belong to Tom Tallyman, and now Blaze and Bo each have the brand too.

'There goes Blaze', shouts Ruby, relieved that the ordeal is over for the little foals. She clambers back up on Muffin to join her dad for the ride home. Flo perks up, glad to see the back of the bully dogs as they're bundled into a truck, and sets off after Ruby.

With her own freshly clipped tail, Merrill shakes free from her rope and escapes from the pound. She's the last to be set loose. With some hurt pride at getting left behind, she starts heading back to her home on Acres Down. But the others have waited for her by the trees and follow on.

Bo trots alongside Faye, keeping one eye on her and his ears to the rear, just in case those horrible dogs are at their heels again. He has had enough excitement for one day.

Ruby's cheeks are rosy as she guides her pony along the lane behind Tom and Connie.
'I'm really proud of Blaze, Dad, she did so well in the drift'. Her voice comes out wobbly as she bounces on Muffin who's trying to keep up with the older mare.

'Ye-es', agrees Tom, with a sideways glance at his daughter. There seems to be a 'but' hovering in his reply.
'She'll be easy to handle in time', he goes on, 'and she's a pretty foal, but -' . Ruby shivers,

scared of what's coming next. '- But you mustn't get too attached to the foals, Ruby. We may not be able to keep them very long. Blaze might have to go to the sales next year and you know the colts can't stay on the forest, so Bo will definitely have to go.'

'But Dad!' Ruby pleads, leaning forward to pull on his jacket sleeve. 'Why can't we bring him onto the farm and break him in for riding? And why can't Blaze live on the Forest with Merrill and Faye and maybe have a foal of her own one day?'

'People are worried about over-grazing, Ruby. There are too many ponies out there - if we're not careful, we'll run out of grass! And while the *subsidy* really helps, we can't afford to keep more ponies on the farm. There's the feed to think of as well as farriers' and vets' bills.'

'Maybe I could help Mum get some extra money - making baskets or candle holders and selling them at the farmers' market - I'd do anything Dad!'

'Well you can start by getting Blaze and Bo used to being around people, and eventually letting us handle them. That will help me a lot and then …. we'll have to see.' And with that he nudges Connie with his heels and they trot briskly away.

Ruby shortens the reins in her hands, thinking hard. She'll enjoy spending more time with the foals but will be really upset if they have to go to the sales next year. She'll have to come up with a plan!

She clicks her tongue and Muffin picks up speed, with Flo sticking close to her tail. They trot together towards the *watersplash*, and beyond is the farmhouse with its tall chimneys merrily puffing out clouds of wood smoke from the fire.

*   *   *   *

After the frightening round up, Blaze and Bo stick even closer together than before. Whenever they hear the sound of hooves pounding at pace across the turf they scatter, always alert.

They're getting to trust the humans, but they like their freedom far too much to be locked up in that pound again!

Can you count how many ponies there are in the pound at Withybed?

6

Newcomers

In the misty Autumn, as leaves fall and the trees' sap goes back down to its roots, spores germinate in the damp soil and something is beginning to grow.

It's mushroom season!

Along the mossy pathways, mushrooms of all different colours and sizes are sprouting everywhere. Blaze jumps when she sees a tall and spiky, cream coloured mushroom sticking up in a place where it hadn't been the week before.

There are yellow mushrooms that look like ears, white mushrooms that look like umbrellas, red toadstools that slugs have bitten chunks out of, and big flat ledges of fungus even growing out of the tree trunks.

With the mushrooms appearing, there's suddenly a lot of humans around too. Carrying bags and baskets, they're on the lookout for mushrooms they'd like to pick, to take home and cook.*

Bo has a nibble of a *penny bun* but doesn't like it at all and spits it out again. The humans are welcome to take their pick - there are plenty of better things for ponies to eat!

But the mushrooms and the foragers aren't the only newcomers to the forest.

A different scent hangs in the air, and Blaze and Bo notice that even the older members of the herd are on tenterhooks. Wherever they stand or graze, an air of agitation settles amongst them, as if they are waiting for an intruder... someone or something that's going to invade their quiet haunt and upset the gentle rhythm of their lives.

And the little green acorns in the trees that bothered Merrill and Faye before have fallen to the ground in their hundreds.

Although the ponies like eating them, they never seem at ease when they're nuzzling the ground under the oak trees. What does it mean?

What can be wrong with the mares? Why does the forest feel strange and dangerous all of a sudden? And then they find out.

With a snuffle and a scuttle the leafy paths of Acres Down come alive with strange noises and smells and then - a sight to make their hooves curl:

ten little white piglets running through the wood grunting, with their pink ears flapping and their wet snouts up in the air bearing shiny metal rings.

The whole herd is thrown into panic and with hooves flying and foals screaming, they scatter. Blaze and Bo don't know which way to turn! They swirl and scurry, throwing up a cloud of earth and leaves at their feet.

And in a split second they're all flying down the track towards the car park to get away from the oncoming army of pigs.

Behind the white piglets, a big sow comes loping along the path. She is huge and grey with big white spots and her ears are the longest and floppiest you could imagine. She grunts and snorts, complaining to the little ones to slow down and not keep leaving her behind.

But the piglets are on a mission - to find and eat as many acorns as they possibly can in the shortest time. They are very greedy and acorns are the sweetest treat to any pig.

From the top of the hill where they stand panting, the ponies watch the strange herd making slow progress along the track. The older mares look knowingly at one another.

They see these squat, hairless animals every Autumn when they're let out onto the forest to eat the fallen acorns. But their appearance and strange smell always unsettles the ponies at the start of the *pannage* season, until they get used to the presence of the newcomers. They don't like these pushy creatures taking over their forest!

The pigs are ignorant of the ponies' fears. Free of the farmer's pigpens for a month or two, they're only interested in finding nice things to eat.

Ponies like acorns too, but they're poisonous for them to eat, so the pigs are doing them a favour by hogging them all, before the little green nuts can give the ponies bad bellyache.

By late afternoon the piglets have moved on and are foraging for acorns in a ditch at the side of the road. Blaze is feeling daring and stalks them at a distance, completely in awe of the smooth white creatures that are so much smaller than her yet so much more fearsome.

Bo trails behind his friend hoping the pigs won't turn around and see Blaze and then chase them both back across the forest. He knows he's not courageous and at the smallest sign of trouble he'll turn tail and run like the wind away to a safe hiding place.

Blaze is creeping dangerously near to the road.

The light is fading as the sun sinks low on the purple horizon. How Bo wishes she would lose interest in the pigs and come back to his side.

Then a new noise reaches the foal's sensitive ears. His eyes swivel in their sockets as a human riding on a bike whizzes out of nowhere making the air rush past him. The brakes squeak loudly, the tyres skid and the man shouts out in surprise.

For a piglet has leapt from the ditch and he swerves his bike quickly to avoid it.

Crash! The cyclist lands upside down in the brambles and the piglets shoot off, squealing in terror. Blaze just misses getting hit by the bike. She bolts into a thicket and by the time she's brave enough to peep out, Bo is nowhere to be seen.

The big sow has caught up with her piglets and leads them all away to safety with a fierce backwards glance at the unfortunate cyclist. The man eventually gets up, all covered in mud and fronds of bracken.

'You just can't predict this place', he mutters, untangling a strand of thorns from his handlebars. 'The forest is full of surprises!'

As he peddles off up the lane in the dim twilight, Blaze realises she's not alone. Faye has come up beside her, looking for Bo. The mare and the little foal scan the horizon with their keen eyes.

Faye nods her wise head and nickers as she suddenly catches sight of Bo's silhouette on the hilltop.

He looks small and lost on the vast dark heath but stands out clearly against the pink sunset.

Blaze senses that Faye will go as far and for as long as she has to, to reach her foal and lead him safely home. And as she has learned to gallop like the wind on the day of the drift, she doesn't waste any time flying off on her spindly legs to help bring Bo home.

Faye watches her streak away across the dusky heath. With her bright blaze shining, she looks like a shooting star!

Some ways of the forest are unpredictable but some will never change. And the loyalty of a herd of wild ponies is one of them.

The wise and knowing mare sets off on her journey, hooves gently clopping on the newly emptied lane.

*Who do you think can go faster - a cyclist or a
galloping pony?*

New Forest vocabulary

Agister - an official who looks after the livestock
    on the forest

Bay - a pony's coat colour which can be light to
dark brown with some black markings

Bog myrtle - an aromatic plant that grows near
marshes and bogs

Briar - a wild bush

Cattle grid - iron grids laid in the ground that
cows and ponies can't walk over

Colt - a young male pony

Commoner - a person who lives in the forest with
rights to graze cattle, pigs and ponies on
common land

Copse - a thicket of small trees

Corral - a fenced pen for holding livestock

Crab fly - a biting insect peculiar to the New
Forest that has a hard shell and moves
sideways like a crab

Drift - the rounding up of ponies to count them
and check their health

Fallow deer - a type of deer that is mainly light brown with white spots

Filly - a young female pony

Flash - the white stripe or blaze on a pony's face

Forage - wild vegetation providing food for ponies and cows

Ford - a place where a natural stream or small river flows across a road

Gorse bush - a prickly bush with yellow flowers that are coconut scented

Goshawk - a large bird of prey

Haunt - the place where a herd of wild ponies spends most of its time

Inclosure - fenced in areas of the forest where trees are grown for timber

Lawns - the grassy areas of the forest which have been grazed by ponies

Muzzle - another name for a pony's nose

New Forest - a 150 square mile National Park in Hampshire providing a natural habitat for many wild animals and species of plants

New Forester - A native New Forest pony

Nicker - a word used to describe the sound of a pony's whinny or neigh

Open forest - the areas of forest that are not fenced and gated

Pannage - the letting out of pigs to forage in Autumn

Peat - a dark brown compost that lies under the forest bogs and can be dug up and dried to burn on fires

Penny bun - a rounded, creamy coloured type of edible mushroom

Pound - another name for the wooden corrals that are used as pens in the Drift

Quarry - animals that are being chased or hunted

Roan - a pony whose coat colour is speckled with white hairs

Subsidy - an amount of money paid to commoners to help maintain their New Forest ponies

Wall eye - an eye that is light blue and lacking the brown pigment of its pair

Watersplash - another name for a ford or stream that crosses a track or lane

Whinny - the high pitched sound a pony makes

Wild boar - a type of pig with a tusk that used to roam in the forest

Witches' circle - mystical man-made rings of broken branches that occasionally appear on the forest floor. They are said to be a gathering place for 'witches' to practice their magical powers.

* Since Autumn 2016, foraging for mushrooms has been discouraged in the New Forest by the authorities in an effort to preserve the different species in their natural habitat.

An extract from
Book 2 - The Yearlings

1

Footprints
in the Snow

Christmas has come and gone. Tanya has taken all the baubles off the Christmas tree and Ruby helps her wrap them in tissue and place them carefully back in their decorations box.

Tom has lit a roaring orange fire in the wood-burner, and the kitchen's warm and toasty.

Through the steamed up windows, the snowflakes can be seen outside floating slowly to the ground. They've been drifting down silently from a black sky all night and have settled in thick layers. Flo's paw prints in the snow are deep and dark.

They lead to a place under the bushes at the end of the garden where Flo remembers hiding her Christmas present - a huge succulent marrow bone which she wanted to bury straight away in a secret place to save for later.

Now she can't remember where she put it!

Soon Ruby appears at the back door dressed in a new wooly hat, wooly scarf and a duffle coat that's just a bit too big for her. It's her favourite surprise from Santa.

She pulls on some cold wellies waiting stiffly by the back door and trudges towards the stable yard.
'You coming, Flo?' she calls, but the old sheepdog is twirling and barking and scratching at the snowy ground here, there and everywhere. She still can't find her bone. She's torn between digging more holes to find it, or going after Ruby.

Tom is in the yard splitting logs with his noisy machine. Crack! and two perfect halves fall to the ground.

'Dad? Can I get some hay to take up to the ponies?' Her dad blows on his hands and his breath makes clouds in the frozen air.

'Sure, they'll be needing it in this weather' he smiles, 'but remember not to get too close to them when they're eating'. He goes to fetch a couple of hay nets to carry it in.

Stuffed full and with stalks trailing out of the big holes, the nets feel heavy slung over Ruby's shoulders. Tom says, 'I know you're sensible enough to go on your own Ruby. If I can trust anyone around the foals its you. And I'm sure they'll soon get to trust you too!'

Ruby's cheeks glow pink. It makes her happy when her Dad says nice things about her. And she knows she's got a knack with the young ponies. She helped break in one of the colts just last year.

But as she carries the hay up towards the hollow her steps are heavy, like her heart. Because once Blaze is used to people and can be brought in to the farm, it will mean that she's ready to go to the pony sales and Ruby dreads that.

Suddenly Flo's there at her side, panting and looking up keenly with one blue eye and one brown one. Her pink tongue that was watering with thoughts of the bone, lolls out hungrily and some snowflakes land on it which makes Ruby laugh.

'Good old Flo! At least we'll never have to let you go!' she says, patting Flo's head with her damp mitten. 'Now we'd better hurry and find those foals - they'll need more to eat than snowflakes!'

......to be continued